淘气的乒乓猫

乒乓猫过生日

〔荷〕米斯·博豪宇斯 著   〔荷〕菲珀·维斯顿多普 绘   蒋佳惠 译

人民文学出版社
PEOPLE'S LITERATURE PUBLISHING HOUSE

夜深了。

It's the middle of the night.

乒乓实在睡不着，因为明天是他的生日。
他会收到什么样的礼物呢?

Pim can't get to sleep because it's his birthday tomorrow.
What will he get?

乒乒希望会有一个非常棒的大蛋糕，外加至少二十份礼物，
因为他邀请了周围所有的猫。

Pim is hoping for a great big cake, and maybe as much as twenty presents
because he has invited all the cats from the neighbourhood.

他再也忍不住了。"乒乒？
你觉得大家都会来吗？我会得到一个很棒的大蛋糕吗？"

He can't keep still any longer. 'Pom, do you think everyone will come?
And that I'll get a great, big cake?'

"女主人总该知道我想要一个很棒的大蛋糕吧，她知道吗？"

'The Lady does know that I want a great big cake, doesn't she?'

"乒乒，乖乖睡觉吧。一切都会很好的。"乓乓说。

'Pim, go to sleep. It will all turn out fine,' says Pom.

可是，乒乒还是不放心。

"哦，对了，乒乒，彩带。你一定要挂彩带哦！"

But Pim is not convinced.

'Oh Pom, the decorations. You've got to hang up decorations!'

"乒乒！"乓乓严肃地说道。

"好吧，"乒乒说，"我已经睡着了。"他紧紧地闭上眼睛。

'Pim!' Pom says strictly.

'Okay,' says Pim. 'I'm already asleep.' And he closes his eyes tightly.

"祝你生日快乐，祝你生日快乐！"
第二天早晨，小鸟唱起了歌。

'Happy birthday to you!'
whistles the little bird the next morning.

"哇噻！"乒乒喊道，
"我过生日啦，我过生日啦！"

'Hurray!' shouts Pim.
'It's my birthday! It's my birthday!'

可是，大家都在哪里呢?

But where is everyone?

哈，女主人来了。

Ha, there's the Lady.

"我亲爱的乒乓，"她说，"生日快乐！"
她挠了挠他的耳朵。

'My darling Pim,' she says.
'Happy birthday!' and she scratches him behind his ears.

女主人把乒乓放到地上，走出门去。"女主人为什么要出门呢？"
乒乓心想，"我们应该一起庆祝我的生日啊！"

The Lady puts Pim back on the floor and leaves the house.
'Why is the Lady going out?' thinks Pim. 'We're supposed to be celebrating my birthday!'

哈，乒乓来了。
"祝你青春永驻，朋友！"说着，他用脑袋蹭了蹭乒乓。
Hey, there's Pom.
'Many happy returns, friend,' he says and he nuzzles up against Pim.

"不过，彩带到底在哪里？"乒乒不安地问道。

"呃，我还有事。"乓乓一边嘟哝，一边匆匆忙忙地离开了走廊。乒乒完全摸不着头脑。

'But where are all the decorations?' Pim asks worriedly.

'Oh yes, I've just got to do something,' Pom mumbles, and he quickly leaves the hallway. Pim is completely puzzled.

看样子，乒乓和女主人根本就不想给乒乒过生日。
他一条彩带、一份礼物也没有见到！

It looks as though Pom and the Lady don't want to celebrate Pim's birthday.
There's not a decoration or a present to be seen!

蛋糕在哪里呢？连个蛋糕都没有！！！

And where is the cake? There isn't even a cake!

门铃响了。

"客人来啦！"乒乒开心地喊道。他冲到门口。

The doorbell rings.
'My guests!' Pim shouts gladly and he runs to the frontdoor.

可是，当乒乓来到门口时，却发现那里一个人也没有。

But when Pim gets to the door, there is no one to be seen.

乒乓没发现牛奶已经送来了。

乒乓赶忙把牛奶瓶提上楼去。

Pim didn't see that the milkman brought small bottles of milk.

Pom quickly carries them up the stairs.

女主人呢？她会带什么礼物呢？
他们是不是想给乒乒一个惊喜？

And the Lady? What is she carrying?
Are they going to surprise Pim?

可怜的乒乓什么也没有留意到。

"这是我过过的最没意思的生日。"他想。

Poor Pim doesn't notice anything.
'This is the worst birthday I've ever had,' he thinks.

"过生日是一件特别激动的事，这特别的日子本该令我开心。
今天终于盼来了生日，可此刻我却感到特别心酸。"

'It's such a fun to have a birthday, a special day that makes me glad.
I've waited so long for my birthday, but now it's here I'm feeling sad.'

"我想要个插着蜡烛的很棒的大蛋糕，吹灭蜡烛许个愿。"

'I want a great big cake with candles, to make a wish and blow them out.'

"还想要又长又美的彩带，和别人的生日一样绚。"

'And lovely coloured decorations. That's what birthdays are about.'

"我还想要朋友们都来开派对，为我唱起快乐的生日歌。
我还能收到许许多多小礼物……哎呀，可没人在此一起欢唱！"

'All my friends come to my party and sing a jolly birthday song.
And then I get a pile of presents... But no one's here to sing along.'

"凯斯，你是来参加我的派对吗？哦，你还带了礼物！
狗骨头？不是送我的？好可惜，我刚才高兴得笑开颜！"

'Fred, have you come for my party? Oh, you've brought a present too!
A dogbone? Oh, it's not for me? I don't know what else to do.'

乒乓喊道："你在那儿干什么呢，凯斯！快上来！"
"那我呢？"乒乒生气地喊道，"今天可是我的生日呢！"

Pom shouts: 'Fred what are you doing there? Come on up.'
'What about me?' says Pim angrily. 'It's my birthday after all!'

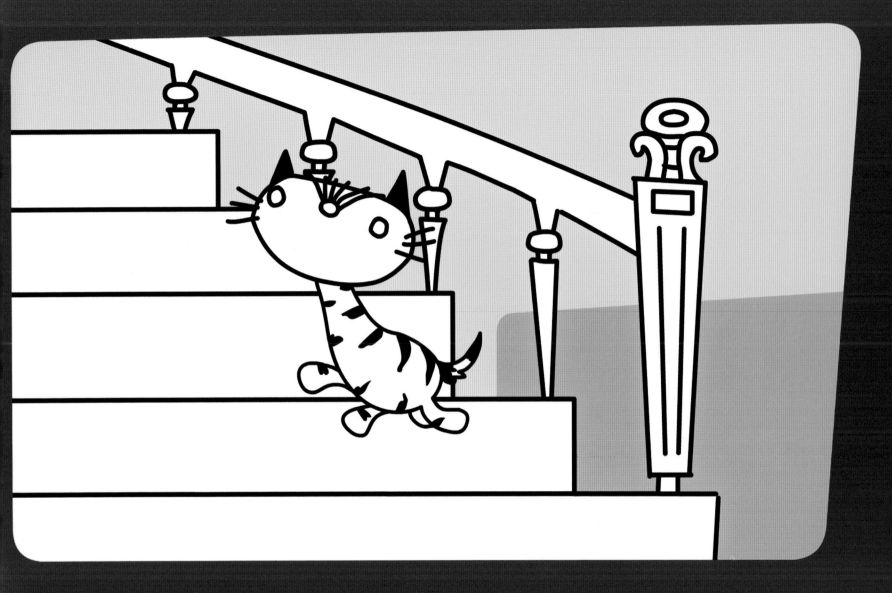

"你为什么不到屋顶上去看一看呢，乒乒？"
"屋顶上？"乒乒一边喊，一边朝楼上跑去。

'Why don't you go and have a look up on the roof, Pim?'
'On the roof?' shouts Pim and he rushes up the stairs.

哇，屋顶上布置得好漂亮啊!
可是，乒乓和凯斯在哪里呢?

Oh, look how beautifully the roof is decorated!
But where are Pom and Fred?

"乒乓？！你在哪儿？"乒乒大声地喊。

'Pom?! where are you?' Pim shouts.

"大惊喜！"所有的朋友齐声喊道。

'Surprise!' shout all the friends together.

他们唱起歌来："祝乒乒生日快乐——！"

And everyone sings: 'Happy Birthday to you, dear Pim. Hurray!'

"这是我过过的最有意思的生日。"乒乒说。

'This is the most wonderful birthday I've ever had,' says Pim.